Filomena's Teachers

Book Four of "The Adventures of Filomena" Series

D1366478

Fernando M. Reimers

I appreciate the helpful feedback and suggestions to a draft of this story
provided by Zohal Atif, Maqui Camejo, Maria Paz Ferrero,
Sofia and Tomas Marcilese, Ishita Ghai, Erin Hayba, Ken Ho,
Nell O'Donnell Weber and Andria Zafirakou

© Fernando M. Reimers

Illustrations: Tanya Yastrebova

Book Layout by Tanya Yastrebova

Library of Congress Control Number:

Kindle Direct Publishing, Seattle, Washington

This book is dedicated to all teachers who help refugee and displaced children feel included and gain the skills to help make a better world

 My name is Filomena. I am a twelve year old parakeet who lives in a small town near the city of Boston. I live with Eleonora and Fernando. They are both professors of education in Universities not far from where we live. As the fall begins each year, they each get ready to teach a new group of students. Once the academic year begins, they each leave home in the morning to go to work and leave my cage on the kitchen table. I listen to music during the day and hear the children in our neighborhood pass by our house on their way to and from school. At the end of the day, I wait excitedly for Eleonora and Fernando to return home from work, so I can learn all about their day as they prepare dinner in the kitchen.

Today I heard them talk in the driveway as they walked up the steps to the back door. The keys tinkled as Fernando opened the kitchen door and came into the kitchen. "Hello Filomena, how was your day? Did you miss us today? You won't believe who I just met today."

"Who did you meet, Fernando?" I replied, as Eleonora came into the kitchen and closed the kitchen door. Fernando understands my chirps and I understand his language, as we have known each other for many years. He speaks to me in English and in Spanish.

"I met the most amazing teacher, Filomena. Her name is Andria Zafirakou. She teaches in the Alperton Community

School in northwest London. She just received an award honoring her good teaching. We had invited her to speak at my University."

"That's nice." I reply with a chirp "And why is Andria such a good teacher?"

"She is an art teacher who teaches in a community school in London. Many of her students moved to London to find a safe home to live. Andria teaches these students to paint. Her students create the most beautiful paintings. I asked her what her hopes are as a teacher. Her answer moved me: she told me that she wants her students to know that she really cares about them, she wants them to be really happy in school, and wants them to paint beautiful paintings, so that other children in school see how wonderful these students are."

"And why did these students leave the countries they were born in?" I ask Fernando.

"They and their families left because it was not safe for them to stay. There are many reasons. Some left because their countries were at war, others because the governments were not treating people fairly, or people were fighting, causing much violence. People leave when they fear their lives are at risk," says Fernando.

"Andria sounds like a kind teacher who loves her students. Do you think I could meet her one day?"

"You sure may, Filomena. I told Andria that I would like to talk to some of her students. We are going to do a web-conference from my computer next week. I could just do that conference from home so that you, too, can meet her and her students. What do you say?"

"I think this is awesome, Fernando. I can't wait!" I chirp with joy.

I was really excited the entire week. I thought of Andria each day, waiting for the time to meet her. The minutes felt like hours, the hours like days, the weekend felt like an eternity. But the day finally arrived. Fernando came to the living room, took the blanket off my

cage and brought me to the kitchen table. Then, he said:

"Good morning, Filomena. Do you know what day it is today?"

"I have been counting the seconds. Today is the day we are going to talk to Andria and her students in London."

"That's right, Filomena. We will do this right after breakfast and before I go to work. It is five hours ahead in London. So it will be right after lunch break when we call Andria.

She will be waiting in front of her computer with some of her students to talk to us."

After breakfast, Fernando moved my cage from one end of the kitchen table and put it next to him. He opened his laptop and connected to the Internet. The Internet would connect us to Andria's laptop in London. The laptop had a camera and a microphone, which would allow Andria and her students to see us and hear us through her computer. Fernando pressed some apps on the computer, and I saw a small window open up. In a small corner of the window, I saw Fernando and the corner of my cage. In a larger window, which filled most of the computer screen, I saw the face of a woman and three young people. I figured they were her students.

"Good morning, Andria. I am here at my kitchen table with Filomena, my parakeet. I told you about her when we met last week in Boston." said Fernando. "I am so looking forward to meeting some of your students."

"Good morning, Fernando, and good morning Filomena. It is nice to meet you." said Andria in an accent I have not heard before. "I am here with my students Massa, Victor, and Zohal. They all read the book 'The Story of Filomena', where Fernando wrote about you, and they have been anxiously waiting to meet you."

"I have been waiting to meet them as well, Andria." I replied, not certain that she or her students would be able to understand my chirps, since I have an American accent.

"Hello, Filomena." said Zohal. "It is nice to meet you indeed. I think it's very nice that you have a family. We also have pets in Afghanistan, where I come from. But we don't have parakeets. Although we do have other kind of birds."

"Hi, Zohal, how nice to meet you." said Fernando. "When did you move to England from Afghanistan? And how do you like being in Ms. Zafirakou's arts class?"

"Hello, Professor. Me and my family left Afghanistan several years ago. When we arrived in England, I did not speak any English. I wanted to make friends but I did not have a way to speak to them. I could speak Pashto very well with my family, but only a few other students in this school speak Pashto. As I was learning English, I also did not speak much, because I was embarrassed that I could not speak as well as most of the other students did. So in the beginning, I just kept to myself. When I enrolled in Ms. Zafirakou's class last year, and she greeted me in Pashto, I was so happy. I soon realized she really didn't speak much Pashto, but she had tried to learn a few words in the many languages which are spoken in the homes of the students in my   school."

"Andria, I did not know you had learned to speak several languages. That's really impressive." said Fernando.

"Well, I wanted to learn about my students and their parents. And I thought it was only fair that I made an effort to speak to them in a language that they love, the language of home, even though it's only a few words. Actually my students quite like that I am making an effort, and they laugh when I make mistakes speaking their language. It helps them see that I am learning too, just like they are. And they like being able to teach me too."

"So, let me hear from another one of you." says Fernando "Tell me Massa, how is it to be Ms. Zafirakou's student?"

"It is very special, Sir. When I am in her class, I know that I am not just an arts student. I am Massa, all of myself. I know Ms. Zafirakou cares about me, about my life. She wants me to be happy. She wants to help me learn. She is like a big sister to me."

"Wow, that's wonderful, Massa. And why is that special? Your other teachers were not like this?" asks Fernando.

"No, Sir, they were not" I began to attend school in Syria, where I was born. When I was only seven, my parents took me and my siblings on a long trip because of the war. We moved to a camp with many other refugees in Jordan. We lived there for seven years, until we were resettled to the United Kingdom. When I came to Ms. Zafirakou's class, I noticed that she started every class spending some time with all of us. She would sit us in a circle and check in to see how we were doing. She asked how things were going in our lives. We do this every day. It doesn't take very long. But it tells us that she is really listening. Sometimes we share things that are going on in our lives that make us feel sad, or confused. Life can be hard sometimes when you have left your home country. And we know it's not just hard for us, but for our parents, too. So it is very comforting to know we have a safe place in school to share and a teacher who cares. It makes me work very hard in her class. I want her to be very proud of me. Can I show you one of the paintings I have done in her class?"

"Please do, Massa. I would love to see your painting.", I said as I flapped my wings. I'm not sure if she understood my chirps, she looked startled. But she opened up a large folder and put it in front of the camera. A beautiful painting of a sunset now filled the screen on our computer.

"Massa, that is just a beautiful sunset!" says Fernando. "I have never seen a sunset like that."

"Well thank you. It is how I remember the sunsets in Syria when I was a little girl.

It was the most beautiful sky in the world.

I painted it because I wanted to give my classmates and my teachers, who have been so good to me, a little bit of Syria. I wanted them to be able to feel the same joy I would feel watching those skies. I have  worked very hard creating this work. It helps me connect with my classmates in ways that words cannot express."

"Victor, and how about you? What can you tell us about Ms. Zafirakou's class?" asked Fernando of the third student, who looked at us sitting in front of the computer in London. He had remained very quiet the entire time.

"All I can say is that in this class it feels like family. Sometimes I think about my childhood in Venezuela, where I came from, and I miss it there.

I know we can't go back because the government would put my father in jail again. He was already in jail for a long time because he was demonstrating so that people could vote freely in elections. But I miss the family that I still have there. I miss my friends. But in Ms. Zafirakou's class I know that I belong. She and the students know me, and care about me. I am not invisible here."

"I understand what you are saying, Victor" says Fernando. "I, too, was born in Venezuela, and know that many people like you and your family have left the country because it was no longer safe for them to live there."

Victor continued "I remember one time when Ms. Zafirakou came to our flat to meet my parents. She does this with many of us. My parents were surprised. We had never been visited by a teacher in our home. That visit made my parents love my school. They ask me about Ms. Zafirakou all the time, because they know she cares about me."

"Andria, you have very good students." says Fernando. "They all say how much they have learned from you. What have you learned from them?

"I have learned so much from them, Fernando. Especially how much hope they and their families have that life can be better. They are all so grateful for the most simple things that make life every day. They appreciate having  each other, food on the table, and the people who have welcomed them in a new country. Learning about a new country can be challenging at times, but my students are very determined and believe that if they study and work hard they can make life better. My students make me feel special, that my work with them matters. I am very grateful to be able to teach them."

"Well, Andria, and Victor and Massa and Zohal. It has been very nice to meet you. I must sign off now because I have to go to work. As you may know we are five hours behind you in Boston, and I must now go to teach my own students. But I am so pleased to have met you all. I think you are all so lucky to be Ms. Zafirakou's students. She is truly a wonderful teacher and I have learned so much from her today. I hope we can talk some other time."

"We would like that very much." said Andria. Fernando clicked on his computer and the screen went off.

We looked at each other, speechless. After a while, Fernando said "Well, Filomena, that is one really good teacher."

I agreed.

Questions for discussion

1. Who is Andria Zafirakou?

2. How did Fernando meet Andria?

3. Why did Filomena want to meet Andria too?

4. How were Filomena and Andria able to communicate between Boston and London?

5. Why did Massa, Victor and Zohal leave the countries where they were born and move to London?

6. How do you think Massa, Victor and Zohal felt when they arrived in London and did not know how to speak English?

7. How do you think other students treated Massa, Victor and Zohal when they had just arrived in London?

8. If you had been in that same school, how would you have treated Massa, Victor and Zohal? Why?

9. What do Massa, Victor and Zohal like about Andria Zafirakou?

10.   What do the parents of Massa, Victor and Zohal think about Ms. Zafirakou? Why?

11. What would you like to tell Massa, Victor and Zohal, if you could talk to them?

12.   What would you like to tell Ms. Zafirakou?

13.   Do you know any people in your community who are refugees? Do you know why they left their home countries?

14.   How do you think people in your community should treat refugees? Why?

The Adventures of Filomena

A series of books to promote intergenerational conversations about values to sustain a world that includes all, available in multiple languages as paperback, kindle and audiobooks

https://theadventuresoffilomena.squarespace.com/

In The Story of Filomena, the first book in the series, Filomena discovers that we all see the world through a frame of mind and that observation is a powerful tool to help us understand how others see the world.

In Filomena's Friends, the second book in the series, Filomena spends many days in the garden during the summer with a diverse group of friends who enrich her life. They discover together how much friends, working together, can achieve.

In Filomena's Seasons, the third book in the series, as the summer winds down, Filomena reflects on the passage of the seasons, and realizes how they punctuate our lives. As she remembers her friend Winter, she discovers that as we spend time with others we become a part of who they are, and they become a part of who we are.

In Filomena's Teachers, the fourth book in the series, Filomena meets a remarkable teacher who teaches arts to children who have left the countries where they were born, with their families, because it was unsafe for them to remain there. Through her care and acknowledgement, this teacher communicates to these students that they are not invisible, and that they belong, and learns how special these students and their families are, and how much they bring to school.

34549606R00018

Made in the USA
Middletown, DE
26 January 2019